Not a Soul but Us

Not a Soul but Us

A Story in 84 Sonnets

RICHARD SMITH

BAUHAN PUBLISHING
PETERBOROUGH NEW HAMPSHIRE
2022

ISBN: 978 0872333604
Library of Congress Cataloging-in-Publication Data
Names: Smith, Richard, 1957- author.
Title: Not a soul but us : a story in 84 sonnets / Richard Smith.
Description: Peterborough, New Hampshire : Bauhan Publishing, 2022. | Includes bibliographical references. |
Summary: "This May Sarton New Hampshire Poetry Prize winning collection brings us to mid-fourteenth century Yorkshire, where the plague pandemic wipes out half the inhabitants of a remote village. Left behind is a twelve-year-old shepherd boy, who with the help of his dog survives near-starvation and a brutal winter and keeps his flock alive. In the months and years that follow, he struggles to reconnect with the life around him. He tells his story in a sequence of eighty-four sonnets—Provided by publisher.
Identifiers: LCCN 2022004224 (print) | LCCN 2022004225 (ebook)
| ISBN 9780872333604 (trade paperback) | ISBN 9780872333611 (ebook)
Subjects: LCGFT: Novels in verse. | Sonnets.
Classification: LCC PS3619.M592463 N68 2022 (print) | LCC PS3619.M592463
   (ebook) | DDC 811/.6--dc23/eng/20220309
LC record available at https://lccn.loc.gov/2022004224
LC ebook record available at https://lccn.loc.gov/2022004225

For information on the May Sarton New Hampshire Poetry Prize:
http://www.bauhanpublishing.com/may-sarton-prize/

Book design by Sarah Bauhan; typeset in Arno Pro with Ellington Pro titles.
Cover design by Henry James
Cover photograph by Peer Lawther.
"The winter fields above Steeton [West Yorkshire]," available on Flickr.com
Author photograph © Steve Behrens

To reach Richard or for more information about the world of the book:
www.richardsmithwriting.com

PO BOX 117 PETERBOROUGH NEW HAMPSHIRE 03458
603-567-4430
WWW.BAUHANPUBLISHING.COM
Follow us on Facebook and Twitter – @bauhanpub

IN MEMORIAM

Richard Earl Smith, 1920–2015

Jean Charlotte Larson Smith, 1926–2018

Deborah Jean Smith LaBoone, 1953–2020

CONTENTS

Yorkshire

AUTUMN

IN THE YEAR OF OUR LORD 1349

1

Our village: plague's been here since summer. Me:
I'm twelve. My family: no one left now. No
more food. Walk: manor: sheepfold: gate. You see
me, wag your tail, bark. The steward turns. "So,
your father?" Nod. "The flock"—he gestures—"you
went with, he taught you?" Nod. He hands me bread.
"Tomorrow, take them up." You herd me to
the barn and paw up hay to make our bed.
I eat, and give you half. You're close all night;
being warm, and touched, reminds me how to sleep.
I dream my father's hands. By the time it's light,
mine know just how to move: palm raised: you leap
up; point: you run outside. What's left to do
but follow? No one's claiming me but you.

2

A half-cut field: the flock can graze here. Yet—
you pause. Flies buzz. There's something rotting. Smears
of blood across his face and hands: the dead
man almost trips me. Then I'm not quite here;
I'm back—two days ago?—that morning, back
at home: *I woke when something smacked my head:*
my father raised the broom—another thwack—
and coughed. Blood sprayed. "Get out." He heaved from bed.
"Don't die with me." He hit and hit. "You're young."
He drove me from the house and blocked the door.
"Set fire to the place," he called, "then run.
You might just live." I stumbled, lay there for
an hour, a night, a day, right where I'd dropped.
His coughing rattled, faded, slowed, paused, stopped.

3

Then I come back to here, this field, the dead
man, you, the flock. It strikes me: we must leave.
We must leave now. I point. You turn your head
and bark the sheep toward home. I wipe my sleeve
across my eyes. My mouth is making sounds
that tell you something's very wrong. Now all
of us—sheep, you, me—go careening down
the hill. I slip and flounder; twice I fall;
but soon we're back inside the fold. I've cut
my hand. You sniff the wound, then lick, your tongue
so slow and soft, it's like—I can't think what,
just something that felt good when I was young.
The bleeding stops, my skin is clean and smooth—
yet you keep licking. I don't want to move.

4

Next morning starts so fine that I forget
to watch the sky. Instead, I think up names
to help me keep track of the sheep: Lisbet,
Aline, Matilda, Walter, Kathryn, James,
Susannah. Then I notice: sleet's begun;
the clouds are low and dark; you're barking from
way up the ridge. I make my count, and one
isn't here. I bark, pursue your answer, come
to where you guard a lamb whose foot got stuck
between two rocks. He bleats and tugs. I hold
him firm and ease him free and bless our luck
we've lost no one. He shakes with fear, or cold.
I pick him up. He settles, tucks his head
in close, and rides me home. Mine Edward. Ned.

5

The church bells haven't chimed for weeks—since June?
July? At first each soul was rung to rest,
till I heard nine in just one afternoon.
The next day: silence. Maybe it seemed best
to keep the number from us. Maybe no
one was alive to ring the bell—just as
no one was left to take the bodies. So
I helped my father carry ours out past
the churchyard to the pit where they got stacked.
One family died together. Neighbors tried
setting fire to that one house. With houses packed
so close, though, flames spread fast: more burned, more died.
But our house stood alone, out on high ground.
It wasn't dangerous to burn it down.

6

The priest says God sent plague to punish sin.
Our first was Hugh, my little brother, two
years old. He burned with fever, half his skin
blue-black, his nose all bloody, screaming through
that night. "What was his sin?" I said. A hiss—
my mother slapped me: "Blasphemy—don't dare—
the Lord will strike—" My father grabbed her wrist:
"Enough!" he warned. She stopped. He stroked my hair.
But she was right. God struck. I'm cursed. I am
a curse. I won't come near a soul but you:
since you're not human, maybe you're not damned
for staying by my side. I hope that's true.
Each morning I wake up before it's light.
You round up all the sheep. We take our flight.

7

We're back by dark. Outside the kitchen there's
a basket where the steward leaves our bread.
I break it: half for morning, half we share
inside the barn before we go to bed.
We lie the way we did when you were small
and didn't have to go and guard the sheep:
your spine against my chest—paws, hands, feet all
mixed up. On some nights, when you're fast asleep,
you dream of running—twitch and whimper till
I rock you. Some nights, my own dreaming wakes
me, leaves me shuddering like I've caught a chill.
You lick my fingers till they do not shake.
And then you lick my palms. And then
my wrists. And then I fall asleep again.

8

The ewes are all in heat. The rams are all
berserk. The oldest clambers awkwardly
onto a ewe who twists away. He falls
off sideways, grunting. Suddenly I see—
recall—*my father, down on hands and knees*
to ape this clown: he'd mount a stool and whack
and poke and pant and thrust and groan and wheeze.
And then he'd play the ewe: bored sigh, glance back,
return to grazing. Mother'd laugh so hard
she'd hide her face—but still the tears streamed through
her fingers. It's just me now, in this yard,
and sheep who don't know they were mocked, and you—
the only thing of mine that isn't gone.
The rams, spent, wander off. The ewes graze on.

9

The morning's misty. House and barn and gate
all fade toward nothing as we walk uphill.
Somebody calls my name, but I don't wait—
I run, and fast, and so do you, until
the voice stops. I'm not sure just why I run—
could be I've kept alone so long that I
have lost the knack for being looked at. Sun
burns off the mist. We find a field that's dry.
I breathe. That night we're quiet as we go
toward the kitchen. Something isn't right:
no waft of smoke, no hum of voices, no
clink-clank of pots, no door-outline of light.
I reach inside the basket, shake my head.
You stare—I think you smell it: there's no bread.

10

I touch the door. It swings wide open. Dark,
and moonlight. Pots strewn. Chairs tipped over like
the people stood up fast. Hearth's cold—no spark.
I find a candle, steel, and flint, and strike
some light. We tiptoe on into the hall—
high-ceilinged, loud with silence. *From outside*
I used to hear men laugh, and sing, and call
each other names, and bang their plates, and fight.
And now I'm inside, in the stillness, you
beside me, passing benches, tables. One
more door: my lord's room. Blankets, pillows, shoes
lie scattered. Packing up to leave was done,
it seems, in one big burst of rush and fuss.
And no one stayed. There's not a soul but us.

11

If someone has the plague, they say, a glance—
one glance—can spread it. That's why no one meets
each other's eyes, and no one takes a chance
on touching anyone. The maggots eat
the face right off a corpse and it just lies
out in the street. A woman carrying
a baby toppled down and died. Her child
lay crying. People just kept hurrying
on past. Next day the child died, too. It's not
just neighbors: folks will leave their husbands, wives,
their children, parents. Most of us have caught
the fear that charity will cost our lives.
That's why I won't go beg. It's not that I'm
too proud. It just would be a waste of time.

12

We backtrack from my lord's room through the hall
into the kitchen. On the hearth I light
a fire. We sleep. At dawn, I ransack all
the cupboards: half a cheese, some salt, a bite
or two of bacon, onions, cabbage, greens,
a leek, beans, oats, stale bread, a turnip, peas.
Into a pot goes half an onion, beans,
oats, water. While it boils, we share some cheese.
The year the harvest failed, my mother'd scant
her bowl. "More to the boy," she'd whisper low
to Father. "Growing fast these days—we can't
stint him." But that was now five years ago.
I'm grown enough. You'll get as much as I
get. Either we both live or we both die.

WINTER

A.D. 1349–1350

13

Each day I shrink our portions. Soon, though, less
is nothing. Search again—still nothing. You
watch everything I do, but I can't guess
how much you understand. Then you walk to
the door and scratch. I open it. You go.
Beyond the fence, you turn to meet my eye.
I nod, not sure if nodding means I know
you're coming back or if we're saying goodbye.
Time passes. Sunlight fades. I sleep. It might
be two days. Then you're here again, and from
your jaw a rabbit's dangling, limp. Your bite's
so gentle I can see no blood. You come
close, open up your mouth. The rabbit drops,
and lies there in a heap. And then it hops.

14

You bark. It hops again. You tap your snout
against its head and grin at me. Its ear
is twitching. I'm not moving. You stretch out
your paw and bat it—playing, as if we're
not starving. You've now done your part, I suppose.
There's no point hating what you've left for me.
I kneel. You watch. The rabbit shakes. I close
my breathing down, and freeze, till I can see
it's dropped its guard. I dart my hand out, seize
its hind legs, lift it high. Its forepaws jerk.
Its mouth gapes, shrieking like a bird that sees
her young being eaten alive. I make fast work:
my free hand grabs the neck and tugs until
it cracks. The rabbit hangs there, quiet, still.

15

The hills—the deep greens—they're all fading. More
and more they're tawny, rusty, patched with white
on colder mornings. We're still hunting for
the green: the ewes seem extra hungry (right
when grass is scarce) and I don't want to use
up all our fodder. We go far afield
each day, off where I've never been, down through
new valleys, up strange hills. The wind's like steel,
and all of us are shivering, though the sheep's
wool's thick and long, and you've grown winter fur,
and I wear three cloaks: none of this can keep
the chill at bay. The only time I'm sure
of warmth is when we sleep—the barn, the hay,
you huddled close. I dream of it all day.

16

You find a field nobody was alive
to harvest. So we graze, then head back through
the silent village. Something happens I've
stopped waiting for: a person that I knew
before steps from a house: a girl I used
to see at church. She carries in her hand
a bundle, which she offers. I'm confused.
"Some bread," she stammers. "Just some spare crusts—and
some cheese." I point to supper swinging from
your jaw. "Your dog"—she smiles—"he feeds you well?"
I nod my head but otherwise am dumb.
"Still—here." She sets the bread down. I can't tell
her thanks—just nod. I wonder, as we walk
toward home, when I stopped knowing how to talk.

17

A heavy snow can make sheep disappear—
the white lost in the white. You track them down;
I brush them off. Far worse than snow I fear
the wind. It blows so thick we almost drown.
It slashes through the densest fleece. It wakes
us in the night: we rush out, drive the sheep
behind a wall, ridge—anything that breaks
the air. I worry we could sleep too deep
and half would die. I'd keep them with us in
the barn, but Father warned me: *"Someplace closed,
the flock, their piss, their breath—the damp begins
to clog their lungs. They're better off exposed."*
But open air's too open. We need more
to choose from. Who are all these buildings for?

18

The chamber—my lord's room—we haven't stepped
inside here since the night we found them gone.
This room—is it still his? Should we have kept
out—that night, now? My mind won't linger on
these questions: my lord's gone till who knows when.
His feather bed, quilts, pillows—I drag all
this through the hall into the kitchen. Then
I go out to the barn, and beat its walls
with anything I find—axe, shovel, stones.
The clay first cracks, then crumbles, tumbles to
the ground. The wattle's left behind like bones
the wind can whistle through. So this will do
for sheep. For us: the kitchen hearth, and doors,
and pillows. I've never slept on one before.

19

One evening, walking home, I see you hop
on three legs, then lie down, then lick your right
front paw. It's cut. I wash it, grip it, stop
the bleeding, wrap a strip of tunic tight
around the wound. I haven't lost my knife,
so I'm not sure what hurt you, till I see
what someone now long dead let drop—a scythe.
That man we once found rotting: he must be
just bones by now. I see you try to stand—
and then give up, just lie there, look at me,
and wait. I kneel and wrap my arms and hands
around you. You don't try to struggle free.
Till now, it's mostly you who's seen us through
all this. Today's my turn to carry you.

20

The days pass, and we eat the last of your
last catch. I pray and hope you'll walk, you'll run,
you'll hunt. You barely limp. I'm waiting for—
for nothing: sure as nightfall, there's no one
who'll come and help us. Round and round inside
my head a thought is circling—hawk above
its prey—and I keep darting side to side
so it won't catch me. I'm not fast enough.
It claws me, sharp and deep, and now I know
what happens next and who does what. We've got
five rams, and one is old, and lame, and slow.
I draw my knife. He's quickly, easily caught.
I drag him round the corner of the yard.
I'll do least harm if I am quick and hard.

21

The ram starts screaming. Like a human: it's
like screams I've heard all year. *A woman shrieked*
inside a dark house. Father rushed in, hit
and swore, chased out a pig. It squealed and squeaked
as Father kicked its bloody snout until
it dropped. We dragged away the man the pig
had tried to eat. His widow wept, too ill
to move. A worse day: with a plague-sore big
and black upon his neck, a man gone mad
with fever ran and jumped into the mill-
pond. Then his sore burst: blood flared like he had
one scarlet wing. He drowned. And then, worse still:
the day my brother's corpse got carried off:
my mother howled—wailed—sobbed—began to cough.

22

The ram keeps screaming, like somebody scared
just half awake by bad dreams. Thick fleece coat—
I grab it, yank him closer. I can't bear
this sound. I rake my knife across his throat
as deep as I can make it go. Blood smacks
the ground like slops heaved from a bucket. I'd
thought he'd die quickly. But he gags and hacks
and gurgles, kicks; his tail flops side to side;
he wheezes. I can feel the life pulse out
of him like someone sobbing. Then he's still,
like he's asleep here in my arms. Without
a sound, you've crept around to see. I'm ill.
I retch. I'm empty. This one, this was James.
I'd best forget I ever gave them names.

23

A dog that bit a sheep—no one would keep
him, he'd be hanged. I slice and peel the hide
clean off; you stand apart and watch. I heap
the guts out on the ground; you still stay wide
of him, as if you can't tell when's the change
from sheep to meat. I try to see just meat—
not him, just it. You keep on acting strange—
fixed, staring, quivering, shifting on your feet
from side to side, as if you want to lunge
but don't yet dare. I realize what it is:
my hands, my forearms, dripping from their plunge
inside his belly. Blood, I'll grant you this.
I stretch my arms out, nod, and you come lick.
I'm glad you do. I want this off me quick.

24

But blood—there's no escaping it. I hack
into his thigh, dig out two chunks of meat.
You snatch one from my hand; I snatch it back
and roast them both, and will not let you eat
until it's cooled. This makes no sense, I know—
you'd love it raw, but we're not brutes. You sniff
the fleece where it lies cast off like a coat.
A coat: I hold it up against me. If
I scrape off all the flesh and cut two holes
to stick my arms through, it will fit. I'll bind
a cord around my waist to keep the cold
out. Still, that leaves the meat and bones behind—
a huge pile, red and gleaming. I forgot
there'd be too much to eat before it'd rot.

25

The mutton that we ate in winter: some
was salty, some was smoky. Scraps of talk—
the cook, my parents—echo to me from
that time and I know what to do: find crocks,
add salt and water, lay in strips of sheep
to soak and cure. The rest I carry to
the smokehouse, drape it on the racks. I keep
the fire there burning low for weeks. And you
and I, we eat now every day. I track
our portions—trying to figure out how long
one ram will keep us both alive. No lack,
no extra—just enough so we'll be strong
and warm. I hope that I won't have to kill
another, hope that this one lasts until—

26

The bread and cheese that girl wrapped up—she'd shaved
off slivers, tithes from every meal. I'd be
ashamed if we didn't pay back what she saved
for us. I bundle up some smoked meat—three
days' worth—and leave it just outside her door.
We turn toward home. The sky hangs dull and thick.
It starts to snow. I try to think no more
about our sins—if they're why folks got sick
and died. Instead, I call to mind what's gone,
what we no longer hear. Dogs barking when
they smelled you pass. The hammer clanging on
the blacksmith's anvil. Mill-wheel grinding. Hens
that clucked. The silly stories Father told.
Then I try not to think. I think of cold.

27

The snow keeps coming—all that day, that night,
next day. I wade out to the barn to feed
the flock. The sheep are standing huddled tight
together; I crawl in among them, breathe
their warmth, am satisfied they're well. I dig
a tunnel in the snow so you can leave
your dirt outside. The drifts have grown so big,
so high, they pen us in: I couldn't heave
myself across one even if I were
full-grown. It's like we're on an island and
the sea's too rough to cross. No need to stir,
though, luckily: the kitchen's like dry land;
there's fire; there's water, food, our bed. The wind
starts pounding on the roof. We settle in.

28

The wind began down low—a rumble. Now
it's adding higher pitches one by one.
It sounds like every soul that died without
a priest to shrive it, unforgiven, shunned
by heaven: all these souls are howling forth
their anguish—anguish that has grown so fierce
that each voice splinters into hundreds—more,
into a thousand voices trying to pierce
God's heart. I wonder why we two've been spared.
I wonder how long we'll be safe inside
this house. How many souls swarm through the air
tonight? Does anybody take their side?
Does what they say just melt away, like snow?
If you and I die here, will someone know?

SPRING

A.D. 1350

29

Susannah is the first. (I shouldn't call
them by their names, I know—but I forget.)
She's sprawled there by the fence, away from all
the other sheep, one hind leg raised, her head
stretched back to watch her belly heave. From out
her backside pokes a sac that looks like snot.
It stretches, thins: I see two toes, a snout.
She stands. She's straining, as if something's not
quite right. I strain with her—it hurts to watch—
but I can hear my father: *"Lad, she's wise
in this. Leave be—our help would only botch
things."* Push, the sac splits, here's the face, the eyes,
the ears—and here's the forelegs. Can he see?
His eyelids rise. He's looking right at me.

30

And now he sneezes. Now he breathes. And now,
now he's alive, himself, though half of him
is still inside the ewe. He stretches down.
Another push: he slides till all four limbs
lie tangled on the ground. He rests. He tries
to stand. His legs are like new flower-stalks
each blown by its own wind. He wobbles, lies
down flat again, then teeters up and walks.
Two steps. Two more. Susannah licks him clean
of blood and muck. You press against my side.
We watch him falter, right himself, then lean
in toward the teat. He finds it, sucks. You stride
off, sniff all round the edges of the yard.
A brand-new soul: there's more for you to guard.

31

Two lambs a day some days, and all are well:
we're adding lives, not taking. Weeks before
they're green, you sniff dry shoots, like you can smell
their roots, their stirring. Sunlight's thicker. More
soft air. Your foot's healed; you catch hares again,
when you're not minding newborns. But today's
a lull: well-stocked larder, quiet sheep-pen.
You sit before me, head high, ears up, gaze
bright, tongue out. We don't often look so straight
at one another. Mostly you're beside
me, like my arm or ear. But now you wait,
your tail wags, you peer right into my eyes.
I've thought all winter I might disappear.
But you still see me. I must still be here.

32

The girl who gave us bread—we pass her by
the church. She stares, a hand raised to her throat.
"I wondered—I'd not seen you since—" she falters. "I
got scared—" She stops. I see her see my coat,
and understand, and glance away. "The meat—
it helped—us—me. Thanks." She looks worried. "When
the lord left—if you'd needed food to eat—
you could have come—" I shake my head. "So then
you've been alone all winter?" "I was not
alone," I try to say, but no sounds come,
just air. So I look down at you, and squat
beside you, close. You gently gnaw my thumb.
"Of course." She sighs, and kneels, and starts to pet
you, like there're things you might help her forget.

33

Aline's in trouble—standing, toiling too
long. I can hear my father: *"Let her be."*
But he's not here. I can't know what he'd do.
It's up to me. I'll reach in, pull it free—
wait, look, here come the nose, toes, ears (they flap),
neck, forelegs, chest. Aline is weary, sways,
falls back—and there's a snap. A quiet snap.
She stands. The lamb just dangles there. The way
his head hangs—it's not right. The rest of him
slides out and drops—a heap. His mother butts
him, licks his face, his belly, all his limbs.
He doesn't move. She bleats, not grasping what's
going on. It's not her fault. She wasn't strong
enough. I stood and watched. I got it wrong.

34

She keeps her vigil. It's turned cold. You bark.
I look: our youngest, Lisbet, has begun
to stamp and strain. She's bleeding—not the dark
thick clots like normal: this is bright red, runs
like water down her legs. A nose pokes out,
but just one leg. The other must be bent,
inside, hoof tearing her. I shove the snout
back in and find the other foot. I meant
to ease it slowly, but it catches, rips
her more—more bleeding. Both the lamb's legs now
are forward. Lisbet pushes, hard. He slips
out, riding on a spate of blood. She bows;
her forelegs buckle; she collapses on
her side. One last loud breath. And then she's gone.

35

The lamb stands up. He sways. I wipe him dry
so he won't freeze, then carry him to where
Aline still nudges at her dead child. I
set down the orphan, hope he'll nurse—but there's
no fooling her: she sniffs—he's not her own—
and backs away. He's shivering, so I fold
my coat around him—coat: I should have known
at once what needed to be done. I hold
him close, scoop up the dead lamb, carry them
around the corner. I'm not sure the dead
one counts as having lived; still, skinning him
feels bad. I make a little jacket—head-
hole, leg-holes—fit it on the orphan. Eat—
he has to—soon—or he'll end up as meat.

36

I put the orphan in his coat beside
Aline. She bends and sniffs—her dead lamb's fleece.
She might ignore him, grieve the one that died,
and let her milk dry up. She might make peace
with any doubt she has and nurse this stand-
in, makeshift child. She might sense makeshift's all
there is. She sniffs again. I press my hand
against the orphan's rump. He takes a small
step, cranes up toward the teat, then wavers—so
I pluck some grass and tickle his behind.
He latches. Aline sighs, stands still, breathes slow;
he sucks, tail wags. Some part of me unwinds,
and I lie down, and fall asleep right here.
I wake when you start snuffling at my ear.

37

I don't get up, just lie and stroke your throat
from underneath. Your fur is soft—black ears,
eyes, back, white chest. It's thick, your winter coat
not shed yet. My two hands don't quite reach clear
around your neck—but far enough that I
could ram my thumbs against your windpipe, stop
your breath. Your jaws—you wouldn't have to try
too hard to snap down on my finger, chop
it off, eat half my arm. But you just play
at nipping. I just rub your belly. You
could bite me, I could choke you, any day:
starvation could have cudgeled us to do
much worse things than it has. We haven't crossed
all lines. We're desperate, but we're not yet lost.

38

I lie here, drowsing, till I hear the flies.
It hits me then: a skinned lamb and a dead
ewe: I forgot, just left them out to lie
uncovered. So I drag poor Lisbet, red
with her own blood, around to where I flayed
the poor lost baby, Aline's boy. There's so
much flesh to carve I'm tired and wish I'd stayed
asleep. But we can't waste this food. I go
away inside me so I won't feel what
I'm doing. First I slice and peel the ewe's
fleece off of her. Another coat. I swat
it to one side and watch her start to ooze.
I'll hack her up and then I'll do the lamb.
Their meat will be more tender than the rams'.

39

One morning I hear ringing—bells. I can
not help but count: a dead child gets one peal;
a woman, six; a man gets nine. The ban
on ringing deaths is past, I guess. I kneel,
in honor to whoever died—but there's
more peals than nine. Perhaps a priest's begun
to ring the hours again as calls to prayer.
I thought this morning, just before the sun
came up, I dreamed bells ringing. Maybe that
wasn't dreaming. Maybe that was matins, first
call of the day. The hours will hammer at
us like they used to: matins, lauds, prime, terce,
then sext, nones, vespers, compline, vigils. I'm
not sure I'll like being back inside God's time.

40

The girl steps from a different house—it's not
where she once gave us bread. She sees me frown.
"My uncle's," she explains. "My parents got—
it happened fast—" Her voice goes thin. "The town—
we had that blizzard—no one came." Tears start,
then stop, as if she willed them back inside.
"And I got blocked in—snow, the door"—my heart
goes numb—"for four days after they both died.
I couldn't sleep. I sat and watched them. Now—"
She shuts her eyes, and something drains away.
She looks at me. "Your name—it's Tom, yes?" How
I do what I do next I cannot say:
I speak: "Yes—Tom." I point to her. "And—Anne?"
She nods. "But call—my parents called me Nan."

41

The wind has brought one last bad storm, and we
have one last ewe to birth. We go to look
for her—our Kathryn. Somehow she broke free
and wandered down the hillside to the brook.
She's dropped her lamb right by the water. Hail
and ice—it's raw. The lamb's not breathing. I
squat down. A girl: she'll freeze soon, she's so frail.
I grab her by the hind legs, lift her high,
and sway her back and forth. Muck drains out through
her mouth and nose. I lay her down and cup
my hands around her snout and breathe into
her, twice, three times. And then her chest heaves up
all on its own. And then it doesn't. Then
it does: up, down, up, down. She's ours again.

42

I tuck her deep inside my coat and rush
toward the kitchen. You herd Kathryn right
behind me. Hearth-stone's hissing: bits of slush
drip from the roof-vent. Fan the coals—they light
back up. More wood, more warmth. A thick cloak: stroke
her back, legs, chest, head, get her blood to stir.
She needs warm stuff inside her, too. I poke
at Kathryn, steer her forward, right to her
new daughter. Then the thing, it happens: lamb
and ewe: they join: the mother feeds the child:
the child is eating. Maybe I'm not damned.
It just might be there's something that has smiled
upon this place, on us. I feel you sigh.
We're both relieved that one more didn't die.

43

I call her Emma. I keep watch: she's nursed
whenever she wants, and Kathryn always bleats
an answer back when Emma calls. The worst
time might be past now: no more snow or sleet;
the pasture's thick with grass and hares, so all
of us can eat. Fifteen new lambs survived;
the flock has twelve more sheep than in the fall.
All ewes we'll keep, but breeding takes just five
rams, so the rest are meat, or fleece, or—but
I don't know who'll decide that now. There's no
one—lord, or steward—no one left. So what's
next? Just me's not enough to make things go
the way they should. The fields—who's going to plow
and plant them? And the sheep—whose are they now?

44

Nan joins us watching sunset from the hill.
You sprawl. She rubs your belly. She says she's
been thinking through how many houses still
stand empty. I look down: from some I see
no thread of smoke. I point. Nan understands
what I am counting, speaks it for me: "Two,
then three, that's five." Then I can't move my hand:
the next no-smoke house I should gesture to
is where her parents died. "I know," she tells
me softly. "Six." We count on: sixteen out
of thirty empty. More than half. The bells
ring vespers. "Wait, the kitchen—didn't you douse
the fire?" She points: the manor. Sky's near black,
but we can see: there's smoke. Have they come back?

45

I herd the flock down to the sheepfold. Light—
a lantern—someone standing. Sheep, you, me—
we all must be just shadows in the night.
"Dear God," the lantern-bearer says. I see
his face—the steward. He comes nearer, shines
it on me. "Christ," he breathes. He sets
the lantern down. It lights us both. My eyes
avoid his; still, it's clear he can't quite yet
grasp this is me. "All winter? You—the sheep—
the dog?" You move in, right against my thigh,
and stiffen. "How'd you eat? How did you keep
alive?" He sees my coat, understands, sighs.
"I called—that day—" His voice begins to crack.
He moves as if to hug me. I step back.

46

He lets me stand apart from him, but he
keeps talking: "Did you hear me call, that day
we left?" I nod. "Then where—why didn't—? We
were leaving, I kept looking, I couldn't stay—
My lord, he panicked. It was stupid. One
cow died—he thought the world was fated to
be drowned in blood, or flames—" He's still not done:
his words spill out like he's confessing. "You
ran off? You were supposed to come away
with us!" I think he means just me alone.
This makes no sense. The flock—you—would have stayed
behind? And I'd have gone—to where, what home?
What life is saved if it's not this life? Who
would I be elsewhere? I'm me here, with you.

SUMMER

A.D. 1350

47

For months, the manor felt like ours. It's not.
The kitchen hearth, where we kept Emma warm—
the cook holds court there once again. We've got
to sleep back in the barn, for now. Men swarm
around, unloading carts and crates. They stare
at me, and some look scared, and others grin;
a few seem troubled. I feel raw, and bare,
and wish that I could step out of my skin
and be like air. The steward finds us, sits
down, motions me to join him, wants to talk.
You sniff him, and he smiles. "You kept your wits
about you," he begins. "You saved the flock.
You fed them, birthed the lambs. You—one dog, one
boy. Just like what your father would have done."

48

"Like what your father would have done," he said.
Since last night, when I saw the smoke with Nan,
each word I've heard feels wrong, and makes me dread
the next, and brace against it. Now this man
has said a different kind of thing. It's more
like something Nan would say, or you, if you
knew how. He doesn't try to touch me or
move closer. He just sits. I listen to
the wind. I stroke your ears. He holds his palm
out, facing up. "My lord sends thanks." Twelve brand-
new coins. They gleam. He waits in patience, calm.
I take them, careful not to touch his hand.
"This is your pay." He clears his throat. "Thank God
you lived, you both." I meet his eyes and nod.

49

Next day a kitchen scullion grabs me: "Time
to wash you, steward says." The barrel's back
behind the barn. I strip down, start to climb
up—but he grabs a shears, begins to hack
my hair off, tugging, nicking. I hold still.
He kicks my clothes aside: "The fire for them."
(My fleece coat's safe—you've dragged it off.) I'm chilled.
Blood trickles from my scalp. It's salty. Then
he hoists me by the armpits, drops me in
the barrel, tries to shove my head down—but
I pull deep fast so he can't touch my skin.
Being here reminds me of—I can't think what
at first, until I look up toward the sky:
my last bath was the day my mother died.

50

She'd lain in bed three nights—huge swellings in
her armpits, coughs you'd think would leave ribs cracked,
her fever making tinder of her skin.
But then her breathing changed, and something clacked
inside her chest. I bent down close. Her face
strained tight, eyes fierce, far-off. Her body shook.
Her breath stopped. She looked past me toward some place
that wasn't there, then lurched bolt upright, hooked
her chin behind my neck, and coughed out her
whole life. It flooded down my back. Then she
lay slack and still against me. I didn't stir.
I didn't want to move, or hear, or see,
or think, or know. My father'd stepped near, had
his arm around her, laid her down. "Good lad."

51

"Good lad," he said again. "Hold still." He drew
his knife and snagged my shirt and tunic back
behind my neck, then slit down—collar to
my waist—till they slid off me. They were black
with Mother's blood. He nudged them with his toe
across the room into the fire. He led
me out the door. I didn't know where he'd go,
but came along. "You're drenched in blood," he said.
"You must get clean." He spoke so soft and slow
it frightened me. He lifted me up high,
then down into our barrel: "There you go."
I closed my mouth, crouched low, and shut my eyes.
This deep, my heartbeat is the only sound.
If I could breathe the water, I'd stay down.

52

That day, my father brought me new clothes. Those,
the scullion burns. The new new clothes I wear
aren't really mine: no one who knows me chose
them, helped me put them on. Last time my hair
got cut was by my mother. But today
a stranger cropped it off. I feel like no
one's: what my family gave's all gone away.
We meet Nan for our walk, up where we go
each evening now. She stares, and then she grins—
"You're shorn!"—and then she peers, and frowns:
"You're cut! There's blood—you're hurt!" Her hand begins
to dart toward my head. She slows it down.
Her fingers don't quite touch what was my hair.
My scalp can sense her hand is almost there.

53

There's grass enough the flock can graze all day
in just one spot. So you and I aren't bound
to watch close: they're so lazy they won't stray.
You trot up to the hilltop, look around
as if to check that all is well, then sprawl
onto your back and wriggle. I stretch out
nearby, then roll and spin and tumble all
the way downhill. You bark and hop about,
play-acting I'm in danger. When I'm still,
you lick my nose, then pant, then whine, then wait.
You're hot and thirsty, but won't move until
I signal you can go squirm through the gate
and splash into the stream. I watch you run.
I lie back, breathe the grass, drink in the sun.

54

Last year, the men who sheared the sheep were calm
and nimble, so the sheep felt rocked, not flung.
They died, those men. These new ones have no qualm
about how much the sheep get tossed and swung
and bruised and gashed. Susannah squirms free, runs
away. Ned kicks the tall one's chin. Aline
keeps twisting from the shears, so she's the one
who's cut worst. Other men come watch the scene,
which makes the shearers fierce—especially
the shorter one. I gather cobwebs from
the barn to stanch the sheep's wounds. Both men see
me working to repair the harm they've done.
The ones who're watching smile, and then it's clear:
the shearers hate me. There'll be trouble here.

55

The short one strides toward me. "Oh, you love
these sheep." He smirks. The men all laugh. The tall
one says, "These little lambs: how many of
them might be yours?" I think, but don't say: *All.*
The laughs turn thick and jagged. I begin
to bob my head and grin: I might be safe
if they believe I'm simple. "It's no sin—
which ewe's your sweetheart?" You go taut, and chafe
at how I grip your collar. "Don't be shy,"
the short one says. "Cat got your tongue?" the tall
one asks me. "Dog, more like." I don't know why
they laugh. The short man backs us to the wall.
I feel you want to lunge, bite, pull him down.
Before you can, he's fallen to the ground.

56

He groans. The steward kicks again, right to
his ribs. Again. Again. He coughs up blood.
The steward grabs the tall one's hood—"Now you"—
and yanks him, shoves him face-down in the mud.
He twines the hood around his neck. "If I
should see a single look"—the tall one gags—
"one sneer at him, his dog, the girl"—the eyes
bulge—"if I hear one word, one breath"—he drags
the man toward his friend—"if I don't like
one thing you do"—he lifts him up, then throws
him down—"you'll rue that you're alive." He strikes
them both again and looks around. "This goes
for all of you." Not one man breathes. "You two,
you'd best just crawl away from here." They do.

57

I've learned if I peer sideways folks don't see
I'm watching. All the men are terrified.
The steward's ashen. No one looks at me.
"Do none of you have work to do?" he chides,
and one by one they slink off. I let go
your collar. He sits down and rubs his eyes.
"You must not play the fool, Tom—never. No
fool could have kept the flock—himself—alive
all winter long. And don't fret—those men, they
won't trouble you again." He looks at me,
and gives me time, and now's when I should say
my thank-you. But my voice is still not free,
not strong, not whole. I'm not sure why. I bow
my head. He nods, like that will do, for now.

58

The steward's warning dug a moat into
the air around us: no one treads too near.
Nan says the same: the men seem scared they'll do
the least thing wrong, speak one harsh word she'll hear.
One day a peddler comes. He lays out all
he has to sell. I've never had a coin
before. I've never bought a thing. He calls
out prices. Suddenly my finger points
to what I want—a knife and whetstone. I'm
surprised but certain. I just had to see
this new knife: all at once it felt like mine;
my old knife had become an enemy.
Two sheep got killed, four skinned: that's what it did.
I'd rather never have to look at it.

59

I find a spade inside the barn and take
it up to where my family lived. Inside
the low stone wall around our yard, I break
the earth and dig down deep enough to hide
the old knife. When it's gone for good, I turn
and glance around. I haven't been here since
last fall. I haven't known just how much burned.
Now, when I see the heap that's left, I wince.
I force myself to look—remember. Here's
the hearth, and here's the pot, the spit, the bake-
stones. Here's the axe-head; here's the scythe-blade; near
them lie some nails, my father's knife. I make
my eyes keep moving. Here's foundation-stones.
Here's where the bed was. Then I see the bones.

60

My father must have woken in the night
and felt death stepping close. He must have thought
through what he'd do: keep still till it was light,
then beat me, drive me from the house. I fought
back. He was strong. "Don't die here with me—walk
away," he called. "First, burn it down." I stayed
outside till all his coughing stopped. He'd blocked
the door, but I pushed through. His body splayed
across the bed as if it were a rag
that's used to mop up blood, then tossed aside.
I knew this house was sick, but couldn't drag
myself away. I had to look. He'd died
eyes open—blank and empty. Nothing shone
there. This was no one I had ever known.

61

Before that day, my father always got
up first and stirred the fire. This once, it would
be me. Beneath the ash, the coals glowed, hot
and red. I fanned them, lit a long stick, stood
up on a stool—and it went out. I laid
the table-cloth across the flame, then caught
it with the stick and raised it. Right away
the roof-thatch flared. I lit another spot,
a third, a fourth. I lit the rushes on
the floor. A burning scrap rose, drifted, lit
my father's clothes, then landed right upon
his face. There should have been some time to sit,
keep watch—but fire was spreading, smoke was thick,
I couldn't breathe. I had to leave here quick.

62

You tiptoe slowly toward what used to be
my father: bones bleached white, his skull half-charred.
You sniff but hesitate, and wait for me
to be the first to touch him. I've tried hard
to lock out all these questions, but they shove
back in: Did fire burn all his flesh? Did wild
beasts finish what was left? Did any of
his bones get carried off? Where are they piled,
and could I find them now? His spirit, must
it wander, howling, through the night—again,
night after night—until he's laid in dust
and someone's prayed for him? The moment when
the burning rushes settled on his head,
was he (oh please, dear God) already dead?

63

My mother and my brother both got blessed
and prayed for, at the grave. As they lay sick,
though, our priest didn't visit—scared, I guess,
he'd catch it. He did anyway. Died quick.
The new priest—he's just Jake the thatcher, who
can no more read than I can. How could he
help Father's soul? I thrust the spade into
the dirt. A deep hole, six feet long and three
feet wide—it's hard, slow work. I study how
his bones lie, carry each one separately,
and set them down just as they had been. Now
is when a priest should speak, but it's just me
and you, and I don't know what words to pray.
"Rest well, now." That's all I can think to say.

64

Some sand would scrub the soot from off the pot—
the tripod, too. The axe-head, scythe-blade—they
just need new handles. Everything that's not
destroyed I want. You sniff and paw your way
through ashes, and we find: A bowl. A jar.
A hinge. Six blackened coins (I never knew
where Father kept them). Scraps of wood beams charred
but firm. I pick one up and cut right through
the singed parts. Then I whittle. It won't take
much time till it's a sheep (once I've begun,
I work fast). Four died, so there's four to make:
one ewe (Lisbet); one newborn (Aline's son);
two rams (the ones I killed so we wouldn't starve).
My new knife's sharp. You sit and watch me carve.

AUTUMN

A.D. 1350

65

Whenever we see Nan, you rush right to
her, tail curled high. She rubs your chest; you sigh;
she ruffles up your neck and head, and you
stretch up to lick her face. She smiles, and I
smile, too. Today I guide her where she has
not walked with us before: our house. She sees
what's burned, what's left. Her face gets tight. Then, as
she strolls and probes and thinks, she's more at ease.
She stops at Father's grave. She waits, stock-still,
then looks around and gathers small white stones.
She lays each one down carefully, until
she's made a cross to mark where Father's bones
lie silent. She steps slowly to my side
and calls you near. "So. Tell me how he died."

66

I clear my throat. "He coughed blood. Yours?" You look
from me to her. "First plague-sores. Here"—she taps
her thigh and armpit—"big as eggs. It took
three days of fever till he died." She wraps
her arms around herself as if she's cold.
You settle close; she strokes you. I begin:
"My mother had those sores. I tried to hold
her when she coughed. She coughed blood on my skin,
all down my back. I held on, felt her die."
My words, like Nan's, feel stony, jagged, true.
She says, "Remembering never stops." Her eyes
go flat. They lighten nothing. Even you
can't make this right. What's gone is always gone.
"And then there was my mother," she goes on.

67

She kneels and trails her fingertip from stone
to stone on Father's grave. "My mother stayed
beside his bed and made me sit alone,
across the room. She bathed his face, and prayed,
and cleaned his vomit. Snow had blocked the door
and windows. All the food, she left with me—
the meat you'd brought, some bread, cheese, not much more.
Some water. Gradually I noticed she
looked bruised. Her nose and mouth bled, hands turned black.
And then she rested. Then my father threw
up blood, all on her face, her hair, her back.
She didn't move. He pulled her close. He knew,
I think. He wept and coughed. Then he was dead,
too. Days passed. Then the door thawed. Then I fled."

68

We sit here by the grave. Nan's finger still
moves stone to stone. "The bruises, blackened skin,"
I say, "that's how my brother—he was ill
one night, next morning died. What was his sin?"
Nan flinches. Then she murmurs, "He did say
plague punished sin. The priest—he said that." We
lock eyes and stare, and we don't look away,
or nod, or shake our heads. We're only free
to not say anything. "Your brother—how
old was he?" I hold up two fingers. "No,"
she breathes. Her eyes were dry, but now
they stream. She doubles over, face hid low.
I touch her spine—and in a rush, I feel
it all: All this—it happened. It's all real.

69

You lick Nan's face until it's dry. My hand
rests on her back. The sun is low, and red;
the whole sky's furrowed pink. She sits up, and
I pull my hand away. Enough's been said,
so we just listen. Wind. Our breathing. I
pull out the sheep I've carved and stand them on
the ground. She takes one. "Perfect little eyes,"
she says. "That's James," I tell her. "This one's John.
And that"—I tap the ewe—"is Lisbet." Nan
leans close to look. "She bled," I say, "I tried—"
Nan waits, then carefully picks up the lamb.
"Who's this?" I shake my head. "No name. He died
when he was born." She nestles him into
my hand. "No, keep him," I say. "He's for you."

70

The three of us still sit. I toss a stone;
it taps against another stone; you bark.
My mind skips back to you and me at home—
right here, when walls and roof and door kept dark-
ness outside all night long. Five years ago
this was: the twins had drowned already; Hugh,
my little brother, wasn't born; and though
we had you, you were still a puppy. You
and I lay close in bed. My parents sat
beside the hearth. You leapt up, cocked your head,
and growled and barked—we didn't know what at.
Then Father gasped: "Fair Folk—Themselves," he said.
"The dog can hear: they're on the road tonight.
We'd best stay safe inside until it's light."

71

"Themselves?" I asked. He whispered, "Fairies! But
don't speak that name: they'll hear you, come for you."
I squirmed and giggled: Father knew just what
to say to make fear tickle. "No, it's true—
your mother, they took her for just one night,
but one night here's a lifetime there." She smacked
him, laughed. "It's why she's pale, thin—not quite right
in the head." "Ha! Me not right—?" "That's just a fact,"
my father said. I asked her, "Where'd they take
you?" "Otherworld," my father said. "But wait—
dogs know that place. He never would forsake
you there. He'd find you, free you, bring you straight
home." I was awed. "He'd come?" "Good Lord above,"
he said, "dogs always save the boys they love."

72

I looked at you with new respect. "He's right,
for once," my mother said. "So there's no call
to fret about these fairies—" "Hush—they might
be listening!" Father warned. She scoffed, "If all
the goblin hordes attacked us, this dog still
could keep us safe." I pressed my face into
your fur and lay there, eyes closed, waiting till
they'd think I'd fallen fast asleep. Then: "You
are daft!" she said. "And wise. If Tom believes
the dog is magic, he will always trust
him." Father said, "That dog will hardly leave
Tom's side. He'd guard him with his life. He must
think Tom's a lamb." They both moved toward the bed.
"That gives my mind a bit of ease," she said.

73

The daylight's draining from the sky, yet we
still linger near my father's grave. Nan looks
at stones, at the foundation, starts to see
things I don't notice. "If"—she stands—"we took
this stone that's over here"—she drags it—"put
it here"—I help her hoist it to the wall—
"it fits." You sniff, and scratch into the soot.
Nan lifts the stone you're pawing. We search all
around the yard, find two more stones that fit,
and settle them where they belong. Somehow,
although it's dark and we should leave, we sit
again, and wait, and listen: us here now,
us three, as if it's where we're meant to be:
just floating on the evening, quiet, free.

A.D. 1354–1357

74

So off and on, for years, we stack that wall
till it comes to your ear. We sweep up soot,
haul off charred wood, and try to make it all
like there had been no fire. Nan helps me put
together what I'll say. I practice till
the words come out without a stumble. Then
I find the steward: "I would like to build
my parents' house back up and once again
live there, if you consent." He's never heard
me speak this many words at one time. He
tries not to look surprised. "But every third
house still stands empty," he begins—then sees
my face and understands. "Of course—your old
house. Once the harvest's in. Before it's cold."

75

Just after Michaelmas, the steward sends
four men each day. We find two houses no
one's lived in since the plague—too wrecked to mend,
though not all posts and beams have rotted. So
we drag the sound ones up the hill and build
upon the stones that Nan and I have laid.
The men grow more at ease with me—less filled
with fear the steward stirred up when he made
his threats. "Now, aren't you Robert's boy?" one asks.
I start—that name sounds strange to me. "You've got
his smile," he says. Another stops his task:
"He's like Joanna, too—that trick of not
quite looking at you but still watching." They
both nod. Those names ring in my mind all day.

76

The posts and beams and rafters make the bones.
The door and shutters fit like armor. Then
comes flesh—more readily put on than stones
or wood, more readily stripped off again:
the walls just mud caked onto woven sticks,
the roof just bundled straw lashed up by Jake.
(They found a priest who hadn't gotten sick
and died; Jake's thatching roofs again.) It takes
two weeks to build the house, two years to save
enough to fill it: blankets, bowls, one cock,
three hens, a cauldron that the steward gave
me, bench, stools, basins, axe, a chest that locks,
two jugs, four spoons, a table, and a cow.
And then I'm done. The house is ready now.

77

What's next takes time. I choose just seven words.
(It's easier with fewer.) Every day
I practice them out loud—to you, the birds,
the sheep, the cow, the hens, the wind. I say
them in my sleep. I carve a boy (or man),
a woman (girl), a dog. One evening, while
we watch the sunset, I take Nan's right hand
and set the carvings out. She starts to smile.
I say: "I'm yours if you will have me." She
goes pale, then flushes. Then she huddles down
against my chest. You nuzzle at her knee.
I slowly bring her closer, arm around
her back. I stroke her hair. I touch her face.
"Lord keep us safe," she says. "God spare this place."

78

Both Nan and I are bound here, to this land,
and to our lord. For us to marry, he
must grant us leave, the priest must read the banns,
and we must pay a fine. We come, we three,
next time the court's in session, to the hall
where you and I crept slow and hushed—eight years
ago, that first night when we'd been left all
alone. No hush today: the whole town's here:
they joke and chatter. Then the steward's clerk
raps on the table. Silence. In my chest,
a huge fist grabs my heart and starts to work
it: clutch, ease, clutch, ease, clutch. Today's a test:
though people here still think I'm simple—weak,
slow, mute—I must step forward. I must speak.

79

The morning's filled with business. Robert Rust
is fined threepence for selling weak ale. John
Hogg swears he did not steal Matilda Cust's
two hens but that she ate them. Simon Bond
agrees. The steward rolls his eyes and fines
her sixpence for her slander. Lambert Long
stole door-posts from his neighbor, Agnes Prine:
he's fined twelvepence; her door must be made strong
again. Joel Wolmer's father died; Joel gets
his land but owes our lord his best cow. Then
it's still. The steward looks around, and lets
a minute pass, and seems about to end
court when I say, "I come to ask my lord's
consent to marry Nan—to wed Anne Ward."

80

The only sound is my own blood inside
my ears. The whole room's staring at me. No
one's heard my voice in all these years. I stride
toward the steward's table. As I go,
some faces soften. Joan Beck nods. She was
my mother's friend—my godmother, I think.
I reach the front, pull out some silver, pause
to count how much I guess I owe. Coins clink
into a stack. The steward stands: "Dear boy"—
he takes my hand—"of course you do not owe
a farthing." He gives back my coins. "All joy
be yours." I bow, turn. Every soul I know
who's still alive is here. It makes me see
how many more of us there used to be.

A.D. 1360

81

You still come out with me to mind the sheep.
You run a little, bark a lot, and dart
at stragglers. Home, you watch our daughter sleep—
eyes fixed, as if you're making sure her heart
is always beating. When she learns to walk,
you're at her side, between her and the fire.
Your name's her first sound that we count as talk
and not just babble. Lately, though, you're tired.
Some afternoons, as we head home, you slow,
and sit, then stand and try, then sit, and look
to me. I scoop you up, and as we go,
you stare, and make your eyes into a crook
that guides the sheep, and they all follow you.
You scarcely walk, and still your work's not through.

82

One day you try to crawl behind the bed,
the chest, beneath the bench. Our daughter laughs
and toddles after you. Nan shakes her head
and meets my eye. We both know you can't last
much longer. All that night I grip you close.
At dawn I wake: you've crawled from bed toward
the hearth. Your breathing rasps and rattles, slows.
I settle in behind you, on the floor,
inhaling how you've always smelled. And then
your breathing stops. Nan hears the silence, draws
near, wraps her arms around us both. And then
I cry. And once that starts, it doesn't pause
until I fall asleep. When I wake up, Nan holds
me still. And I hold you. By now, you're cold.

83

Nan's planted Father's grave with flowers. Just
nearby's a bare spot, where I dig. Nan comes
out with our daughter, who looks scared. She must
face sorrow in her life, I know that. Some
things, things her parents saw, I hope she's spared.
But this one can't be helped. "Come say goodbye,"
I call. She stares at you: "Is he still there?"
I kneel down with her. "That's his body," I
say softly, "but his soul has flown off." She
looks up. "He'll still be watching out for you,"
Nan says. That soothes her. I dig deeper—three,
four, five feet. Cradling you, I slide into
the hole. The next thing I can hardly bear:
I have to lay you down and leave you there.

84

I climb back up and toss down earth by hand.
I think of how my life's been saved—more ways,
more times, than I will ever know: *My Nan,*
who always waits on what I have to say.
My mother, who went hungry so that I'd
grow strong. The steward, who has housed me, fed
me, paid me, shielded me. My father died
alone in hope I'd live. My parents said
you'd brave the fairies so I'd trust you. You—
above all, you—you took me on when I
had nothing, I was nothing. Soil sifts through
my hands. It aches, how fast this all goes by:
I lose you more each time I scatter on
more dirt. Your paws. Tail. Shoulder. Nose. Ear. Gone.

ACKNOWLEDGMENTS

I owe big debts of gratitude to:

Meg Kearney, for honoring my work with this award and for understanding and commending it so beautifully.

The team at Bauhan Publishing—Sarah Bauhan, Mary Ann Faughnan, Joal Hetherington, Henry James—for shepherding this book into public view with expertise, care, and kindness.

The actors at the American Shakespeare Center in Staunton, Virginia, whose performances over the years have tutored my ear in the expressive possibilities of iambic pentameter.

These dear longtime friends who read early drafts and encouraged me along: Charlotte Armstrong, Billy Aronson, Becky Bailey, Elizabeth Cheng, Keller Easterling, David Groff, Michelle Hensley, Steve Holland, and Gary Krist.

Above all: my beloved partner of thirty-eight years, Steve Behrens, and our beloved dogs, Barney and Jennie. You three save my life every day.

BIBLIOGRAPHY

Aberth, John. *The Black Death: The Great Mortality of 1348–1350*. New York: Palgrave Macmillan, 2005. Kindle.

Ackroyd, Peter. *Foundation: The History of England from Its Earliest Beginnings to the Tudors*. New York: Thomas Dunne Books/St. Martin's Press, 2011. Apple Books.

Alcock, Nat, and Dan Miles. *The Medieval Peasant House in Midland England*. Philadelphia: Oxbow Books, 2013.

Armstrong, Dorsey. *The Black Death: The World's Most Devastating Plague*. Audio lecture series. Chantilly, VA: The Great Courses/The Teaching Company, 2016.

Armstrong, Dorsey. *Turning Points in Medieval History*. Audio lecture series. Chantilly, VA: The Great Courses/The Teaching Company, 2012.

Atkin, Malcolm, and Ken Tompkins. *Revealing Lost Villages: Wharram Percy*. London: Historic Buildings and Monuments Commission for England, 1986.

Benedictow, Ole J. *The Black Death, 1346–1353: The Complete History*. Woodbridge, UK: Boydell Press, 2004.

Bennett, H. S. *Life on the English Manor: A Study of Peasant Conditions, 1150–1400*. Cambridge: Cambridge University Press, 1937 (first paperback edition, 1960).

Beresford, Maurice, and John Hurst. *Wharram Percy: Deserted Medieval Village*. London: B. T. Batsford /English Heritage, 1990.

The Black Death: A History from Beginning to End. Hourly History, 2016. Kindle.

Boccaccio, Giovanni. *The Decameron.* Translated by Wayne A. Rebhorn. New York: Norton, 2013. Apple Books.

Brooks, Geraldine. *Year of Wonders: A Novel of the Plague.* New York: Penguin Books, 2001. Apple Books.

Cantor, Norman F. *In the Wake of the Plague: The Black Death and the World It Made.* New York: Free Press, 2001.

Carroll, Carleton W., and Lois Hawley Wilson, trans. and eds. *The Medieval Shepherd: Jean de Brie's Le Bon Berger (1379).* Tempe, AZ: Arizona Center for Medieval and Renaissance Studies, 2012.

Chapelot, Jean, and Robert Fossier. *The Village and House in the Middle Ages.* Translated by Henry Cleere. Berkeley: University of California Press, 1980, 1985.

Daileader, Philip. *Late Middle Ages.* Audio lecture series. Chantilly, VA: The Great Courses/The Teaching Company, 2007.

Daimler, Morgan. *Fairies: A Guide to the Celtic Fair Folk.* Winchester, UK: Moon Books, 2017. Kindle.

Defoe, Daniel. *A Journal of the Plague Year, Written by a Citizen Who Continued All the While in London, During the Last Great Visitation in 1665.* London, 1722. Kindle.

Elliott, Lynn. *Clothing in the Middle Ages.* New York: Crabtree, 2004.

Emery, Anthony. *Discovering Medieval Houses in England and Wales.* Princes Risborough, UK: Shire Publications, 2007.

Forest, Danu. *The Druid Shaman: Exploring the Celtic Otherworld.* Winchester, UK: Moon Books, 2013.

Gies, Frances, and Joseph Gies. *Life in a Medieval Village*. New York: Harper & Row, 1990. Apple Books.

Hanawalt, Barbara A. *The Ties That Bound: Peasant Families in Medieval England*. New York: Oxford University Press, 1986.

Hatcher, John. *Plague, Population and the English Economy, 1348–1530*. London: Macmillan, 1977.

Hatcher, John. *The Black Death: A Personal History*. Philadelphia: Da Capo Press, 2008. Apple Books.

Hinds, Kathryn. *Medieval England*. New York: Benchmark Books, 2002.

Holmes, George. *The Later Middle Ages: 1272–1485*. New York: Norton, 1962.

Horrox, Rosemary, trans. and ed. *The Black Death*. New York: Manchester University Press, 1994.

Hudson, William Henry. *A Shepherd's Life: Impressions of the South Wiltshire Downs*. Originally published in 1910. Apple Books.

Jillings, Karen. *Scotland's Black Death: The Foul Death of the English*. Stroud, UK: Tempus, 2003.

Kelly, John. *The Great Mortality: An Intimate History of the Black Death, the Most Devastating Plague of All Time*. New York: HarperCollins, 2005. Apple Books.

Kenyon, Sherrilyn. *The Writer's Guide to Everyday Life in the Middle Ages*. N.p.: Writer's Digest Books, 1995. Apple Books.

MacLeod, Sharon Paice. *Celtic Cosmology and the Otherworld: Mythic Origins, Sovereignty and Liminality*. Jefferson, NC: McFarland, 2018. Kindle.

Manchester, William. *A World Lit Only by Fire: The Medieval Mind and the Renaissance; Portrait of an Age*. New York: Little, Brown, 1992. Apple Books.

McNeil, Heather. *The Celtic Breeze: Stories of the Otherworld from Scotland, Ireland, and Wales*. Englewood, CO: Libraries Unlimited, 2001.

Mortimer, Ian. *The Time Traveler's Guide to Medieval England: A Handbook for Visitors to the Fourteenth Century*. New York: Touchstone/Simon & Schuster, 2008. Kindle.

Mount, Toni. *Everyday Life in Medieval London: From the Anglo-Saxons to the Tudors*. Stroud, UK: Amberley, 2014. Apple Books.

Paxton, Jennifer. *The Story of Medieval England: From King Arthur to the Tudor Conquest*. Audio lecture series. Chantilly, VA: The Great Courses/The Teaching Company, 2010.

Piponnier, Francoise, and Perrine Mane. *Dress in the Middle Ages*. Translated by Caroline Beamish. New Haven: Yale University Press, 1997.

Platt, Colin. *King Death: The Black Death and Its Aftermath in Late-Medieval England*. Toronto: University of Toronto Press, 1996.

Rebanks, James. *The Shepherd's Life: Modern Dispatches from an Ancient Landscape*. New York: Flatiron Books, 2015. Apple Books.

Ruiz, Teofilo F. *Medieval Europe: Crisis and Renewal*. Audio lecture series. Chantilly, VA: The Great Courses/The Teaching Company, 1996.

Singman, Jeffrey L. *The Middle Ages: Everyday Life in Medieval Europe*. New York: Sterling, 2013.

Steindl-Rast, David, and Sharon Lebell. *Music of Silence: A Sacred Journey through the Hours of the Day*. Berkeley, CA: Seastone, 1998.

Stroud, Kevin. *The History of English Podcast* (2012–present). Especially: Episode 83: "A Trilingual Nation"; Episode 110: "Dyed in the Wool"; Episode 117: "What's in a Name?"; Episode 118: "Trade Names"; Episode 120: "The End of the World." https://historyofenglishpodcast.com/episodes/.

Tuchman, Barbara W. *A Distant Mirror: The Calamitous 14th Century*. New York: Random House, 1978. Apple Books.

Walker-Meikle, Kathleen. *Medieval Dogs*. London: British Library, 2013.

Willis, Connie. *Doomsday Book*. New York: Bantam Books, 1992. Apple Books.

Ziegler, Philip. *The Black Death*. New York: HarperCollins, 2009 (originally published by the John Day Company, 1969).

The May Sarton New Hampshire Poetry Prize

The May Sarton New Hampshire Poetry Prize is named for May Sarton, the renowned novelist, memoirist, poet, and feminist (1912–1995) who lived for many years in Nelson, New Hampshire, not far from Peterborough, home of William L. Bauhan Publishing. In 1967, she approached Bauhan and asked him to publish her book of poetry, *As Does New Hampshire*. She wrote the collection to celebrate the bicentennial of Nelson, and dedicated it to the residents of the town.

May Sarton was a prolific writer of poetry, novels, and perhaps what she is best known for—nonfiction on growing older (*Recovering: A Journal*, *Journal of Solitude*, among others). She considered herself a poet first, though, and in honor of that and to celebrate the centenary of her birth in 2012, Sarah Bauhan, who inherited her father's small publishing company, launched the prize. (www.bauhanpublishing.com/may-sarton-prize)

PAST MAY SARTON WINNERS:

In *The Wreck of Birds*, the first winner of Bauhan Publishing's May Sarton New Hampshire Poetry Prize, Rebecca Givens Rolland embraces an assimilation of internal feeling and thought with circumstances of the natural world and the conflicts and triumphs of our human endeavors. Here, we discover a language that seeks to at once replicate and transcend experiences of loss and disaster, and together with the poet "we hope that such bold fates will not forget us." Even at the speaker's most vulnerable moments, when "Each word we'd spoken / scowls back, mirrored in barrels of wind" these personal poems insist on renewal. With daring honesty and formal skill, *The Wreck of Birds* achieves a revelatory otherness—what Keats called the "soul-making task" of poetry.

> —Walter E. Butts, New Hampshire Poet Laureate (2009–2013), and author of *Cathedral of Nervous Horses: New and Selected Poems,* and *Sunday Evening at the Stardust Café*

Rebecca Givens Rolland is a speech-language pathologist and doctoral student at the Harvard Graduate School of Education. Her poetry has previously appeared in journals including *Colorado Review, American Letters & Commentary, Denver Quarterly, Witness, and the Cincinnati Review,* and she is the recipient of the Andrew W. Mellon Fellowship, the Clapp Fellowship from Yale University, an Academy of American Poets Prize, and the Dana Award.

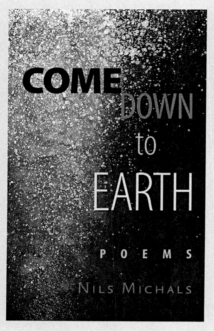

Nils Michals won the second May Sarton New Hampshire Poetry Prize in 2012, and has also written the book *Lure*, which won the Lena-Miles Wever Todd award in 2004. His poetry has been featured in *The Bacon Review*, *diode*, *White Whale Review*, *Bay Poetics*, *The Laurel Review* and *Sonora Review*. He lives in Santa Cruz, California and teaches at West Valley College.

Nils Michals is alternately healed and wounded by the tension between the timeless machinations of humankind and the modern machinery that lifts us beyond—and plunges us back to—our all-too-human, earthly selves. Supported by minimally narrative, page-oriented forms, his poems transcribe poetry's intangibles—love, loss, hope, a sense of the holy—in a language located somewhere between devotional and raw, but they mourn and celebrate as much of what is surreal in today's news as of what is familiar in the universal mysteries . . . *Come Down to Earth* is a 'long villa with every door thrown open'"

—Alice B. Fogel, New Hampshire Poet Laureate (2014-2019), and author of *Strange Terrain: A Poetry Handbook for The Reluctant Reader* and *Be That Empty*

David Koehn won the third May Sarton New Hampshire Poetry Prize in 2013. His poetry and translations were previously collected in two chapbooks, *Tunic*, (speCt! books 2013) a small collection of some of his translations of *Catullus*, and *Coil* (University of Alaska, 1998), winner of the Midnight Sun Chapbook Contest. He lives with his family in Pleasanton, California.

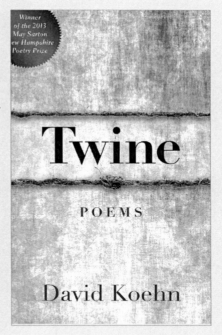

David Koehn's first book, *Twine*, never falters—one strong poem after another. This is the work of a mature poet. His use of detail is not only precise and evocative; it's transformative."
—JEFF FRIEDMAN, 2013 May Sarton New Hampshire Poetry Prize judge and author of *Pretenders*

David Koehn's imagination, rambunctious and abundant, keeps its footing: a sense of balance like his description of fishing: "Feeling the weight . . . of the measurement of air." That sense of weight and air, rhythm and fact, the ethereal and the brutal, animates images like boxers of the bare-fist era: "Hippo-bellied/And bitter, bulbous in their bestiary masks." An original and distinctively musical poet.

—ROBERT PINSKY,
United States Poet Laureate, 1997-2000 and author of *Selected Poems*, among numerous other collections

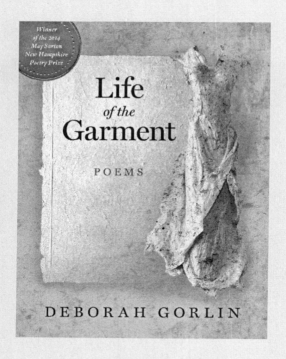

Deborah Gorlin won the 2014 May Sarton New Hampshire Poetry Prize. She has published in *Poetry, Antioch Review, American Poetry Review, Seneca Review, The Massachusetts Review, The Harvard Review, Green Mountains Review, Bomb, Connecticut Review, Women's Review of Books, New England Review,* and *Best Spiritual Writing 2000.* Gorlin also won the 1996 White Pine Poetry Press Prize for her first book of poems, *Bodily Course.* She holds an MFA from the University of California/Irvine. Since 1991, she has taught writing at Hampshire College, where she serves as co-director of the Writing Program. She is currently a poetry editor at *The Massachusetts Review.*

In poem after poem in *Life of the Garment,* Deborah Gorlin clothes us in her fabric of sung words, with characters unique and familiar, and facsimiles of love that open and close their eyes, comfort, and gaze upon us. Read this fine collection—you will see for yourself.

—Gary Margolis, 2014 May Sarton New Hampshire Poetry Prize judge and author of *Raking the Winter Leaves.*

Desirée Alvarez won the 2015 May Sarton New Hampshire Poetry Prize. She is a poet and painter who has received numerous awards for her written and visual work, including the Glenna Luschei Award from *Prairie Schooner*, the Robert D. Richardson Non-Fiction Award from *Denver Quarterly*, and the Willard L. Metcalf Award from the American Academy of Arts and Letters. She has published in *Poetry*, *Boston Review*, and *The Iowa Review*, and received fellowships from Yaddo, Poets House, and New York Foundation for the

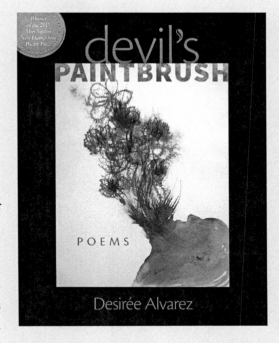

Arts. Alvarez received her MFA from School of Visual Arts and BA from Wesleyan University. Testing the boundaries of image and language through interdisciplinary work, as a visual poet she exhibits widely and teaches at CUNY, The Juilliard School, and Artists Space.

These poems often shot shivers up my spine. Some made me cry. This is a book I'll want to read over and over.

—Mekeel McBride, 2015 May Sarton New Hampshire Poetry Prize judge and author of *Dog Star Delicatessen: New and Selected Poems*

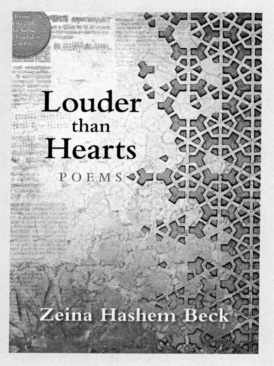

Zeina Hashem Beck won the 2016 May Sarton New Hampshire Poetry Prize. *Louder than Hearts* melds English and Arabic, focusing on language throughout.

Beck is a Lebanese poet. Her first collection, *To Live in Autumn*, won the 2013 Backwaters Prize; her chapbook, *3arabi Song* (2016), won the 2016 Rattle Chapbook Prize, and her chapbook, *There Was and How Much There Was* (2016), was a smith|doorstop Laureate's Choice, selected by Carol Ann Duffy. Her work has won Best of the Net, been nominated for the Pushcart Prize, the Forward Prize, and appeared in *Ploughshares*, *Poetry*, and *The Rialto*, among others. She lives in Dubai and performs her poetry both in the Middle East and internationally.

"I don't know how Zeina Hashem Beck is able to do this. Her poems feel like whole worlds. Potent conversations with the self, the soul, the many landscapes of being, and the news that confounds us all—her poems weave two languages into a perfect fabric of presence, with an almost mystical sense of pacing and power."

–Naomi Shihab Nye

Jen Town won the 2017 May Sarton New Hampshire Poetry Prize. *The Light of What Comes After* is an autobiographical mosaic of memory and dreams that speaks to all of us trying to make some semblance of aging and what it means to live well. Jen Town's poetry has appeared in *Mid-American Review, Cimarron Review, Epoch, Third Coast, Lake Effect, Crab Orchard Review, Unsplendid, Bellingham Review,* and others. Born in Dunkirk, New York and growing up in Erie, Pennsylvania, Town went on to earn her MFA in Creative Writing from The Ohio State University in 2008. She lives in Columbus, Ohio, with her wife, Carrie.

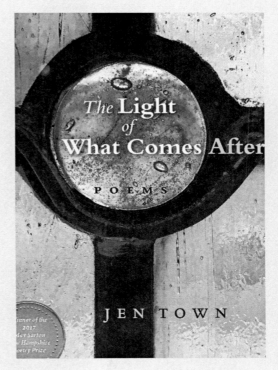

"*The Light of What Comes After* offers a sure manifesto against the domestic and cosmetic. Town's rich linguistic moments and surprising imagery lend her voice a slant which can seem playful and unafraid, but warning is always stitched just below the surface. This is a writer who knows 'Your debts / are more than you'll ever pay back.'"

–– Jennifer Militello, 2017 May Sarton New Hampshire Poetry Prize judge and author of *A Camouflage of Specimens and Garments*

MARILEE RICHARDS

The Double Zero

POEMS

Marilee Richards won the 2018 May Sarton New Hampshire Poetry Prize. Richards learned poetry from Charles Entrekin and others after she wandered into a workshop put on by the Berkeley, CA, Poet's Co-op in the eighties while working as an adoption interviewer for Alameda County. Richards attended the workshops for several years prior to the organization dissolving and her move to Arizona in 2001. Her poems have been published in many journals, including *The Yale Review*, *The Southern Review*, *Rattle*, *Poetry Northwest*, *The Journal*, and *The Sun*. She is the author of *A Common Ancestor* (Hip Pocket Press, 2000), and in 2016 she won the William Matthews Poetry Prize.

This is a poet with range—sympathies, anger, tragedy, other people, love, humor. . . . Richards writes unsentimental poems that road-trip through our times and look around at who is with us when we stop to fill up our cars at gas stations, [who] has been with us in offices . . . she reminds us of what the country has gained in consciousness and freedom, . . . what sorrows and suicides we have left necessarily behind, as the bus pulls up at the curb in the don't-you-get-it-yet years we have been motoring through lately.

—David Blair, judge of the 2018 May Sarton New Hampshire Poetry Prize, and author of *Friends with Dogs* and *Arsonville*

Dorsey Craft is a PhD candidate in poetry at Florida State University. In addition to winning the May Sarton New Hampshire Poetry Prize, she has published her first chapbook, *The Pirate Anne Bonny Dances the Tarantella*, (Cutbank, 2020). Her work has appeared in *Colorado Review, Crab Orchard Review, Greensboro Review, Massachusetts Review, Ninth Letter, Passages North, Poetry Daily, Southern Indiana Review, Thrush Poetry Journal* and elsewhere. She holds an MFA in poetry from McNeese State University and is the Poetry Editor for *The Southeast Review*.

You will love Dorsey Craft's rollicking persona, pirate Anne Bonny, who serves up heaps of scintillant treasures from the bottomless trunk of her imagination, wit, and verve. In *Plunder*, Jack Sparrow has met his match.

—Deb Gorlin, judge, 2019 May Sarton New Hampshire Poetry Prize, and author of *Life of the Garment*.

In *Plunder* Dorsey Craft creates a ripple in the time-space continuum and brings 17th century pirate Anne Bonny to the 21st century. In these intense and erotic poems Bonny's wild and passionate life finds a place in the heart and mind of a contemporary woman and her struggle for love and freedom. This is a luminous and lyric debut.

—Barbara Hamby, author of *Bird Odyssey*

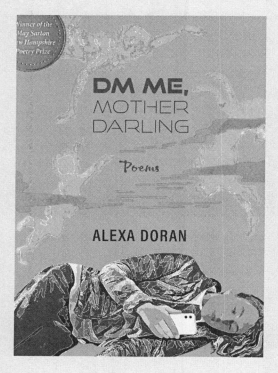

ALEXA DORAN is the 2020 winner of the May Sarton New Hampshire Poetry Prizeand is the author of the chapbook, *Nightsink, Faucet Me a Lullaby* (Bottlecap Press 2019). She is currently a PhD candidate at Florida State University.

Her series of poems about the women of Dada, "The Octopus Breath on Her Neck," was recently released as part of Oxidant/Engine's BoxSet Series Vol 2.

You can also look for work from Doran in recent or issues of *Los Angeles Review, Mud Season Review, Salamander, Pithead Chapel* and *New Delta Review*, among others. She lives with her son in Tallahassee, Florida

Alexa Doran's *DM Me, Mother Darling* begins with a quote from J. M. Barrie's *Peter Pan*, in which little Michael asks his mother, "Can anything harm us?" Throughout the book, Mother Darling, who has lost her children, and the mother of a young boy, who tries to prepare her son for the world, speak to this seemingly ordinary question. However, as titles such as "Mother Darling Smokes a Spliff" and "For My Son, Who Asks Me to Replay Lizzo's 'Juice'" suggest, Doran casts these two women in wildly imaginative and compelling scenarios. The result is a book full of wit and wisdom. I can't recall the last time that a debut poetry collection made me laugh so hard or filled me with such surprise and wonder.

—Blas Falconer, author of *Forgive the Body This Failure*